One sunny summer day as Liberty started her new school, she woke up with anticipation and excitement. Liberty was looking forward to making new friends and meeting her new teacher.

She picked out her favorite pair of shoes to wear and a new blue dress, her favorite color, of course!

As Liberty began to eat breakfast, she began to get nervous. Her mom noticed that she began to stop eating and asked, "Liberty, are you okay hunni bunni bear?" What's wrong?" Liberty said, "Mom, what if the kids who don't know me stare?"

Her mom replied," Always remember Mommie loves you, and God made us all different, and that's okay!" Her mom reassured Liberty, "It's okay to be different, to be uniquely you!" Liberty smiled, hugged her mom, and headed for the school bus.

"Hurry up, Oliver; you're going to be late, "mom yelled. Oliver is Liberty's brother.

"Here I come, mom," said Oliver as he rushes down the steps, kisses his mom, and heads for the school bus.

"Liberty, wait for me," he yells. "Hurry up, Oliver," shouted Liberty. "You're going to make us miss the bus!" As Liberty and Oliver stepped on the bus, they see tons of familiar faces and some new ones, too!

The bus pulls up to Parker Elementary, where Liberty is in sixth grade, and Oliver is in eighth grade. "Have a good day, Liberty," Oliver yells after he rushes off the bus to a group of his friends that he hasn't seen all summer.

"Here goes nothing," she says to herself. As Liberty exits the bus, she sees her best friends Ava and Lucy. This made her a little less nervous about walking into her new classroom.

The three girls found their lockers, put their bookbags in, and headed to room 507. They walked in and greeted their new sixth grade teacher, Mr. Phillips.

Mr. Phillips greeted the girls with a cheerful, "Hello,"
and requests that they find their seats, and so they did.
In comes 10 new students to the classroom this year.

Mr. Phillips rings the bell to get everyone's attention. "Alright, class," he begins. "Let's all take a second to stand one by one and introduce ourselves."

Liberty starts to sweat and hopes she is not called first. "Ava, let's start with you," says Mr.Phillips. "Tell the class your name, your favorite color, and what you did over the summer," said Mr. Phillips.

"My name is Ava McHenry, and my favorite color is pink. Over the summer, I spent a lot of time with my family. We played games, had water balloon fights, and made slime."

"That's awesome," said Mr.Phillips. "Who wants to go next," asked Mr. Phillips. "I'll go," said Nathan, one of the new boys in the class.

"My name is Nathan Baxter, and my favorite color is green. This summer, my family and I went camping and made s'mores, and when we woke up, there was a bear outside of our tent eating our food!"

Everyone in the class said, "Whoa," and then Nathan said, "Sike," and the class began to laugh. "Okay, class, that's enough," said Mr. Phillips. "Who's next?" Liberty, how about you," he said.

Liberty swallows the lump in her throat, stands up, and begins.

"Hi!" My name is Liberty McNeil, and my favorite color is royal blue, like my dress and shoes. Over the summer, my family and I went to Hawaii, took pictures of volcanoes, and swam in the bluest ocean in the world."

Liberty got so excited reliving her summer, she was no longer hiding her hand. All of a sudden, Nathan, the new kid, blurts out, "What's wrong with her hand!" He continues, "Did her fingers get cut off in the ocean?"

Liberty's heart drops, and she immediately sits down. "That's enough," yelled Mr.Phillips. The lunch bell rang, and everyone packed up and headed to lunch.

"Don't worry about him, Liberty," said Ava. "Yeah," said Lucy. "You're just as special as any of us." "Thanks, guys," said Liberty. The school day soon ends, and Oliver and Liberty meet on the school bus to head home.

"Why the long face?" asks Oliver. "I hate school," Liberty said, with tears in her eyes. "Every time I meet someone new, they make me feel like I'm a weirdo because I was born with three fingers instead of five," Liberty said sobbing.

As Oliver leans over and hugs Liberty, he asks, "Do you know how to swim?" "Of course, I do," said Liberty. He asks, "Can you ride a bike?" "Of course, I can. I'm the fastest bike rider in town!"

Oliver asks, "Well, what can't you do?" "I can do anything," said Liberty. "Exactly," said Oliver. "You can do the same things anyone else can do! God made you in your own unique and special way!"

Never let anyone make you feel like you're weird or not special. We're ALL special in God's eyes.

As Liberty and Oliver exited the bus and walked home, their mom was patiently waiting on the porch. "How was school you two?" asked mom.